Top game
play on YOUR next
road trip...

THE COUNTRY GAME

This game can be played in a group of any size.

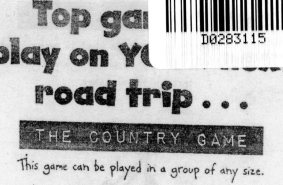

HOW TO PLAY:

1. One player is selected to go first and they have to name a country. The next player will then have to name a place that starts with the last letter of the first country. For example: player one says Greece, player two says Egypt, player three says Turkey and so on...

2. If a player takes longer than ten seconds to think of a country name they will be eliminated. The game will continue until a player can't think of a country. The last person to name a country is the champion!

Find more fun and games at
www.wimpykidclub.co.uk

ALPHABET PACKING

The aim of this game is to decide what to pack to take on holiday from player to player, going right through the alphabet.

HOW TO PLAY:

1. Player one thinks of an item to pack beginning with an 'A' and says, for example: 'I went on holiday and I packed an Armband.' The second player carries the tale on by naming an object beginning with 'B': 'I went on holiday and I packed an Armband and a Bucket.' On it goes: 'I went on holiday and I packed an Armband, a Bucket and a Camera' . . . until (if you're all clever enough) you get to 'Z'.

2. Each item must have something to do with holidays, packing or travelling. Any player who fails to think of a suitable object within a short time limit (say, five seconds) must drop out. The last person to name a country is the champion!

Find more fun and games at
www.wimpykidclub.co.uk

THE WIMPY KID ROAD TRIP TRIVIA GAME

How well do you know the *Diary of a Wimpy Kid* books? Test yourself against your friends and family with this tricky quiz. Answers are at the bottom of the page – no peeking!

1. Who does Greg try to impress by the pool in *Dog Days*?

2. What is the name of the book club that Greg's mom sets up in *Dog Days*? **a)** Reading is Cool, **b)** Reading is Fun, **c)** Reading is Awesome

3. Why was Greg trapped indoors with his family during the Christmas holidays in *Cabin Fever*?

4. In *The Ugly Truth*, Greg's school announces a special fundraiser for the music programme called a ___?

5. True or false: Rowley felt really sick after riding the Cranium Shaker in *Dog Days*.

6. Who wins 'Athlete of the Month' in book one?

7. Where did Rowley go on holiday in *Rodrick Rules*?

8. What's the name of the lawn-care company that Greg and Rowley start in *Dog Days*? **a)** V.I.P. Lawn Service, **b)** Mowers 'R' Us, **c)** Gardeners Inc.

9. What do the Heffleys name their dog in *Dog Days*?

10. What did Manny shoot out of his nose when Greg made him laugh in the car in *Rodrick Rules* (GROSS!)?

More questions on the next page!

Find more fun and games at
www.wimpykidclub.co.uk

THE WIMPY KID
ROAD TRIP TRIVIA GAME

More questions to test your Wimpy Kid knowledge.
Answers are at the bottom of the page - no peeking!

11. True or false: Greg's pen pal is named Mamadou.

12. In which book did Mom and Dad go away and leave
Greg and Rodrick in charge for the night?

13. How many people had to share the ice-cream cone that
Mrs Jefferson bought while on holiday in *Dog Days*?
a) One, **b)** Six, **c)** Four

14. True or false: Mom has a Teddy Cuddles
bumper sticker on her car.

15. Where did Greg and Rowley's family stay
during their holiday in *Dog Days*?
a) Noisy Beach, **b)** Tranquil Lake, **c)** Quiet Cove

16. What does Greg use to take his books to school in *Hard Luck*?

17. What is the name of Rowley's comic strip
that becomes a catchphrase?

18. In what type of transport does Greg want to arrive
at the big Valentine's Dance in *The Last Straw*?

19. Why didn't Greg, Rodrick and their dad stay at the campsite
at the end of *The Last Straw*? **a)** There was a bear attack,
b) It was raining, **c)** There were too many spiders

20. Why did Greg pass the geography exam
really easily in book one?

Find more fun and games at
www.wimpykidclub.co.uk

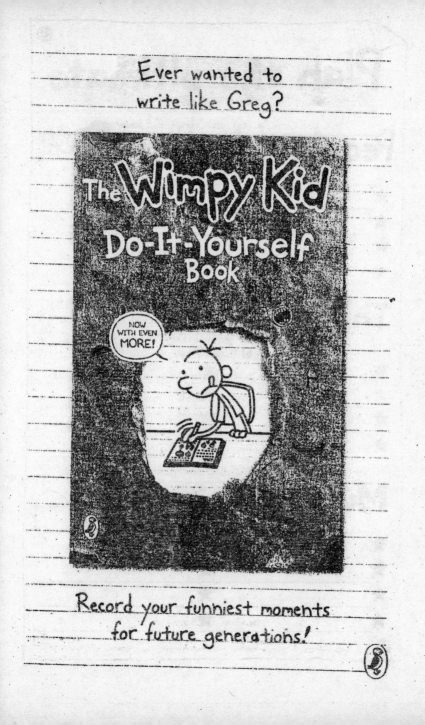

Plan the ultimate

People to invite

* _____
* _____
* _____
* _____

Things to pack

* _____   * _____
* _____   * _____
* _____   * _____
* _____   * _____

Music to bring

* _____   * _____
* _____   * _____
* _____   * _____
* _____   * _____

ROAD TRIP

Places to see

* ★   ★
* ★   ★
* ★   ★
* ★   ★

Map your route

Design your own

DON'T FORGET BUNK BEDS, COUCHES, A KITCHEN,
A BATHROOM, TELEVISIONS AND ANYTHING ELSE
YOU'LL NEED FOR LIFE ON THE ROAD!

Dad had to circle the parking lot about ten times, which wasn't easy since we were towing a boat. Eventually, Rodrick came out with a couple of bags of groceries. And, from the looks of it, he picked up some extra items for himself.

When Dad pulled the van round, Rodrick hopped in. Then we started looking for a place to stay for the night, but the selection in the area wasn't that great.

A few of the motels had big signs that said they had "Colour TV", which if you ask me is not anything to brag about in this day and age.

Dad finally pulled over at a place with air-conditioning and a pool, which sounded pretty good to me, especially considering that I'd lost about five pounds in sweat sitting in the back seat.

I haven't stayed in a whole lot of motels, but, if I had to guess, I'd say we picked one on the lower end of the spectrum.

The lobby smelled like mildew, and the carpet was covered in weird stains.

But everyone was too tired to get back in the car and look for another place to stay.

We got the key to our room, and when we walked in it reeked of smoke. There were little holes in the covers and pillows that I'm pretty sure were cigarette burns.

Dad picked a towel up off the floor, then dropped it because it was WET.

Mom went back to the front desk and asked for a different room, but the clerk said the motel was full and that we'd got the last one.

Mom told her in that case we were gonna leave and take our business to another motel. But the clerk told her there was a twenty-four-hour cancellation policy, so we couldn't get our money back.

When Mom returned to the room, she said we were gonna have to try to make the best of a bad situation. Then she and Dad stripped the bed down to the bare mattress.

Believe it or not, Manny slept through ALL of this. Mom said that if he woke up now he'd be awake all night, so she was just gonna let him sleep through till morning.

Mom put Manny down in the middle of the sofa bed and pulled a blanket over him.

The rest of us were really hungry, so we emptied out the groceries Rodrick bought. But it turned out he didn't buy ANYTHING on Mom's list.

Rodrick was supposed to get sandwich supplies, orange juice and stuff like that, but he just got a bunch of things HE likes.

Mom was pretty upset that Rodrick didn't get a single thing on the list she gave him, but his excuse was that he couldn't read her handwriting. Mom told him it wasn't very smart to get cinnamon rolls and a frozen pizza, since those things needed an oven and we didn't HAVE one.

But Rodrick said we could MICROWAVE the pizza. Then he put it inside the microwave oven to prove it.

At least, Rodrick THOUGHT it was a microwave. It was actually a SAFE. By the time he figured that out, the pizza was locked inside.

Mom gave me what was left of her cash and said to go down to the vending machine to get the most nutritious stuff I could find.

And that's how we ended up eating sugar wafers and breath mints for dinner on the first night of our road trip.

Sunday

Last night we couldn't watch TV or do anything in the room because Manny was asleep on the pullout sofa.

Mom wouldn't even let us keep the light on, so we all sat in the dark for a while until me and Rodrick decided to go down to the pool to kill some time.

Well, the sign outside the motel said there was a pool, but there was no actual WATER in it.

And it didn't look like there HAD been for at
least five years.

There was a hot tub near the pool that DID have
water in it, but some family was already using it.
So me and Rodrick waited our turn.

Unfortunately, the family couldn't take a hint that we wanted to use the hot tub, so eventually me and Rodrick just went back to the room.

The lights were still out, and Mom and Dad were asleep on the mattress. I guess they must've been pretty exhausted, because they were still wearing all their clothes.

With Mom and Dad on the bed and Manny on the sofa, it didn't leave a lot of good sleep options for me and Rodrick.

We checked the closet for a cot or an air mattress, but there was nothing.

Rodrick was one step ahead of me, though. He gathered up the sofa cushions and made a bed for himself on the floor. Five seconds later, he was out cold.

I figured the closet was as good a place as any for me to sleep, so I got some towels out of the bathroom and laid them on the floor.

After lying there for a minute, I noticed a TERRIBLE smell and thought a mouse must've died in the vent or something.

I tried covering my nose with a washcloth, but that seemed to make the smell even WORSE.

It was hard enough trying to fall asleep under those conditions, but then someone in the room started SNORING. Luckily, I was prepared for that. Mom and Dad BOTH snore, which is the reason I thought ahead and brought earplugs on the trip.

But it was so dark in the room I could only find ONE in my duffel bag, so I had to try sleeping with the earplug in my left ear and my other ear pressed to the floor.

I did actually fall asleep for a few minutes, but woke up to some kind of ruckus going on outside.

When I looked out of the peephole, I saw something flash by, but I couldn't tell what it was. So I cracked open the door to see what was going on.

It turns out those kids from the hot tub had got their hands on a cleaning cart and were ramming it into a wall.

I couldn't BELIEVE these kids' parents were letting them run wild in the middle of the night, so I stepped out of the room and went over to give them a piece of my mind.

The littlest kid burst into tears and ran into his room, and I didn't feel bad for even one second. But a minute later his door opened again, and his FATHER came out.

I wasn't about to get yelled at by a grown man in his underwear, so I ran back to our room and locked the door. Then I prayed with all my might that the chain lock was strong enough to keep him out.

I guess the kids' dad didn't see which door I went into, because he knocked on the wrong one. Then he pounded on the door right next to ours before giving up and going back to his room.

Once the coast was clear, I hung a little sign on our doorknob in case the guy decided to come BACK.

It was REALLY hard falling asleep after that, because every time I heard someone outside the door I held my breath until they passed by.

Before I knew it, the sun was up and so was Manny. Mom turned on the television, and whenever Manny watches TV he TALKS to it.

I was a little annoyed with Manny blabbering away, but I guess I can't complain. I used to do the same exact thing when I was younger.

One time when I was watching my favourite show, the host asked a question.

I was just goofing around when I answered, but the guy on TV actually RESPONDED.

OK, POLKA DOTS IT IS!

I wish it never happened, though. Because for a long time after that I thought the people inside the TV could hear everything I said.

AND HOW ARE YOU TODAY?

I COULD BE BETTER. MY BROTHER RODRICK—

THAT'S GREAT!

In fact, on my sixth birthday, Mom had to sit me down and have a talk about the difference between "imaginary" friends and "real" friends.

HEY, DID YOU HAPPEN TO SEE WHAT MY PARENTS GOT ME? IT'S A BIKE, ISN'T IT? BLINK ONCE IF THE ANSWER IS YES!

Once Manny got going in a conversation with his favourite TV characters this morning, I knew there was no point in trying to fall back asleep. So I just got up for the day.

And, when I did, I found out the source of that awful smell. Rodrick had put his shoes in the closet, and I had spent the whole night breathing in his fumes.

But even WORSE was that the "washcloth" I had used to block the smell was actually one of Rodrick's SOCKS.

Speaking of Rodrick, Manny's conversation with the TV didn't bother him one little bit, because he just slept right through all the noise.

CAN YOU HOP LIKE A FROG?

HOP! HOP!

ZZZZ

Dad was getting a little restless waiting for everyone to get going this morning. He's one of those guys who gets up every day at the crack of dawn so he can arrive at his office early, and this whole late-start thing wasn't working for him.

Eventually, Mom made Rodrick get up and take a shower. We went to a diner right next to the motel for breakfast, then got back in the van.

Mom said that from now on we were all gonna be on the same sleep schedule so we wouldn't waste any more time on our trip. But, before she was even done talking, Manny passed out in his car seat.

Mom's big plan for the day was for us to go to a country fair she read about in "Family Frolic".

I'd never been to anything like that before, but it looked like it was worth checking out.

HIGHWAY 1
130TH ANNUAL
COUNTRY FAIR
#1
FOR
FAMILY FUN!
FOOD! CONTESTS! PRIZES!

The fair was a few hours away, so that meant me being cramped in the back seat again, which was starting to get old. Thankfully, after an hour, Mom offered to switch places with me.

When I got up to the front seat, I couldn't believe how much ROOM there was.

And it wasn't just all the space that was awesome. I even had individual temperature settings and my own cup holder.

I went to change the radio station, but Dad stopped me. He said only the DRIVER gets to pick the music. I didn't think that was fair, but I wasn't gonna complain and risk getting sent to the back seat.

MY TRUCK IS BUSTED BUT MY DOG HE LOVES ME

Dad's music was pretty awful, but the view totally made up for it.

When you're in the back, you don't have any sense of what's ahead. Sitting up front, I had a whole new perspective and could almost see why Mom was so gung ho about taking this road trip.

When we took the exit for the country fair, we came to a stoplight. We were behind a minivan that was the same exact model as ours, only purple.

The kids in the van looked kind of familiar. It took me a second to realize they were the same ones from last night.

I hadn't told Mom and Dad about the incident with the kids and the cleaning cart, because I was worried I wouldn't come out looking too great. And they definitely didn't need to know about my run-in with Mr Beardo.

The kids in the purple van recognized me right away and started making obnoxious faces.

I wasn't gonna just sit there and take it from those little punks, so I made a face at THEM.

The skinny one made the same face back at ME, and the second he did the light turned green and they accelerated. When their van lurched forward, the little kid face-planted into the back window.

Dad passed them on the left, and Mr Beardo got a good look at me.

Luckily, the parking lot for the fair was only a few hundred feet up the road. Once we stopped, I wanted to stay inside until I was sure we weren't being tailed by the purple van.

But it looked like we were in the clear. Manny was still asleep in his car seat, so Mom said she'd stay back with him and the rest of us could go on ahead.

The fair was a LOT different than I thought it was gonna be. I expected it to have a Ferris wheel and a merry-go-round and stuff like that, but instead there were a bunch of tents with farm animals and booths with homemade food.

We were getting kind of hungry anyway, so we went looking for something to eat.

They had corn dogs and doughnuts and all the stuff you'd expect at a big fair. But then they had crazy things like deep-fried butter on a stick.

I was actually glad Mom was still in the van, because I was pretty sure that kind of thing didn't qualify as "real food" in her book.

After about an hour of walking the fairgrounds, Dad went back to the car to see if Manny was awake yet, and he told me and Rodrick to go explore on our own.

The two of us wandered around for a while until we came across a tent where there was something big going on.

It was a Foulest Footwear contest, and they were offering a prize for whoever had the nastiest shoe.

There was a big line of people ready to submit
their entries.

FOULEST FOOTWEAR
CONTEST

I told Rodrick HE should enter, because if
ANYONE deserved to win this thing, it was him.

While we were waiting in line, me and Rodrick got
in an argument over who would get to keep the
prize. I said we should split it 50-50 because it
was my idea, but he said he should get the whole
thing because it was HIS shoe and he was the one
who made it stink.

Right before we got to the judging table, we reached a compromise where I'd get 10% of the prize as Rodrick's agent.

Some of the other shoes looked a lot worse than Rodrick's, and I was losing confidence that he'd win. But when the judges got to the smell test it was all over.

Rodrick won first prize, which turned out to be a coupon for one deep-fried butter on a stick. I told Rodrick he could have it all to himself, because the thought of eating any more butter made me feel a little nauseous.

Rodrick asked the judges for his shoe back, but they said they were gonna send it on to the national competition. So that left Rodrick walking around with only one shoe. I decided to explore the nearby stalls while Rodrick was polishing off his stick of fried butter.

But I had a SERIOUSLY close call when I turned a corner and almost ran smack into the entire Beardo family. Luckily, I was able to duck for cover just in time.

Now that I knew the Beardos were on the fairgrounds, I was eager to get out of there.

I went to look for Rodrick, but he must've gone back to the van. I decided to head there myself, but on my way out I spotted the top of Mom's head in a crowd under one of the livestock tents.

People were packed shoulder to shoulder, and I tried pushing my way through to get to where Mom was.

But, when I got halfway in, a big cheer went up.

When I finally made it up to the front, I was surprised to see Manny standing in the middle of the crowd, holding a piece of paper.

Apparently, there was a contest to see who could come the closest to guessing the weight of a hog, and Manny got it exactly right.

The prize for guessing the hog's weight was a real live baby pig.

Mom explained to the judge that they'd just entered the contest for fun and didn't actually WANT the pig.

But the people in the crowd seemed kind of insulted and wouldn't take no for an answer.

With all the commotion this was causing, I was nervous the Beardo family was gonna come over to the livestock tent to see what was going on. Luckily, by then Mom seemed ready to get out of there herself, and we made our way to the exit.

Dad was sitting in the van with the air-conditioning cranked up, and when he saw Mom carrying a pig he was a little taken by surprise.

Mom filled Dad in on how Manny won the pig in the contest, but he didn't seem too thrilled with the news.

Dad said we had no business owning a pig and that we needed to take it back to the fair immediately.

But Mom said it was too late, because the pig had already "imprinted" on Manny.

Dad still wasn't on board, though. He said a pig is a "barn animal" and could be carrying all sorts of parasites and whatnot. But Mom said a LOT of people keep pigs as pets, and she'd heard they're just as smart as dogs.

Then Rodrick got in on the conversation. He voted for KEEPING the pig because he said we could get free bacon from it every morning, the way you get eggs from a chicken.

So either he doesn't understand how pigs work, or he just wasn't thinking it all the way through.

I was all in favour of keeping the pig if it meant we could hurry up and get going.

I noticed a purple van parked a few spaces away from ours, and I was nervous the Beardos would show up any second.

Dad finally caved in. He said if we were gonna keep the pig it would have to ride in the boat. But Mom said putting the pig in the boat was "inhumane" and that we needed to find a place for it in the van.

The thing is there wasn't anywhere to PUT the pig in the van. We couldn't just let it roam free, and we couldn't exactly strap it in with a seat belt, either. So Mom emptied out the cooler and put the pig in THERE.

Once that was settled, we finally pulled out of the parking lot.

After we put a few miles between us and the fair, I could finally breathe again.

But the pig started causing trouble right away. By the time we got back on the highway it had tipped over the cooler and was rooting around in one of the Mommy Meal bags.

I had to wrangle the pig back into the cooler, and THIS time I strapped the seat belt across it so it wouldn't tip over.

Mom figured the pig was hungry, so she said we needed to stop and get it some food. Her idea was for us to go to a restaurant and then give the pig our leftovers. That sounded like a good deal to me, since it meant we'd actually get to have a sit-down dinner.

We found a place to eat a few miles away, and Mom stayed back in the van with the pig while the rest of us went inside. But when the waitress saw that Rodrick was only wearing one shoe she said she couldn't serve him.

Dad said me and Rodrick could take turns using MY shoe. But I wish I hadn't let Rodrick go first, because he's the world's slowest eater.

When we got back in the van, we gave the pig our leftover corn and vegetables, which it ate straight out of the styrofoam container.

Mom started looking up places to stay for the night on the GPS. She asked Rodrick to call a hotel to see if they had any rooms available. They did, but Rodrick blew it by getting too specific.

THEY SAY, "NO PIGS."

Mom found another place a few miles away, and this time she did the talking.

The hotel was just after the tolls. A few hundred feet from the exit, traffic came to a crawl.

That was a problem for me because I had two
big glasses of lemonade at the restaurant and
REALLY needed to use the bathroom.

I spotted a petrol station up ahead and asked
Mom and Dad if I could hop out and use the
bathroom, then catch up with the car after I
was done.

Dad didn't like the idea because he was worried
that by the time I got back they might already
be through the tollbooth. By now it was pretty
obvious the pig needed to go, too, because it was
running in little circles inside the cooler.

Mom said I could use the bathroom at the petrol
station as long as I brought the pig WITH me.

So I tucked it under my arm and ran across three lanes of traffic to the petrol station.

I tried the handle to the men's room, but it was locked. I waited for the person using it to come OUT, but whoever was in there wasn't in any rush to wrap things up.

I was getting kind of desperate, so I tried the handle to the women's room, but THAT was locked, too.

I ran back to the car, which had only moved forward about five feet in the time I was gone.

When I told Mom that both bathrooms were occupied, she said petrol-station bathrooms are ALWAYS locked and that I had to ask the ATTENDANT for the key.

So I ran BACK to the petrol station and told the guy at the desk I needed to use the restroom in a hurry.

I'm not sure what I was expecting from a petrol-station bathroom, but it was actually a lot WORSE than I could've even imagined.

Let me just say it was pretty awkward using the toilet with a farm animal staring right at me. But the pig was even MORE embarrassed than I was, because when it was the pig's turn to go nothing happened.

After I gave the key back to the attendant,
I spotted our van just as it was about to go
through the tollbooth. So I sprinted all the way
across traffic to get to it in time.

But, before I opened the door, I wish I
had noticed that the van didn't have a BOAT
attached to it.

OUR van was actually still a few cars back and,
by the time I got inside, the pig looked like he
was about to burst.

I guess Mom was right about pigs being smart,
because when I put him on Manny's potty seat
he knew EXACTLY what to do.

Monday

When we pulled up to the hotel last night, I was relieved that it looked a lot nicer than the place we stayed the night BEFORE.

Mom and Dad weren't taking any chances on getting turned away at the desk because of the pig, so we kept it in the cooler until we got into our room.

SNUFFLE GRUNT

I think Mom felt bad about the sleep situation at the motel the first night, because this time she rented TWO rooms so everyone would have a bed.

But I should've known there was a catch. Mom said, since she and Dad had Manny in THEIR room, the pig was gonna have to stay in OURS.

I didn't know what I was supposed to do with the pig, so I tried putting it in our bathtub. But it started whimpering the second I set it down.

I decided to let the pig loose in the bathroom, but when I peeked inside a few minutes later it had made a TERRIBLE mess in there. And I'm pretty sure it ate a bar of soap, too.

I let the pig free in the bedroom so I could keep an eye on it, but the first thing it did was go straight to the door connecting the two rooms.

Eventually, Dad got sick of all the noise and opened the door to let the pig in.

I was so tired I fell asleep before my head hit the pillow.

This morning I woke up to the sound of weird noises coming from the foot of my bed. At first I thought Rodrick had got up early, but then I realized the sound was coming from the PIG.

GOBBLE CHEW CHOMP

It had somehow figured out how to open the minibar door and was rooting through the candy and other snacks inside.

I picked the pig up and put it in our bathtub, then went next door to tell Mom and Dad what happened. But it turned out the pig had raided THEIR minibar, too.

Somehow it had even got into the DRINKS. I counted at least three empty cans on the floor, and don't even ask me how a pig managed to do THAT.

Dad went down to the front desk to tell them our "pet" had got into the minibar and we shouldn't be charged for all the stuff it ate.

But the clerk told Dad we were gonna have to pay for the stuff from the minibar and, on top of THAT, there was a fifty-dollar penalty for violating the hotel's "no pet" policy.

After the final tally, the pig ended up costing us more than the ROOMS did.

Mom was eager to get on the road, so she woke Rodrick up and told him to get in the shower. But I probably should've mentioned to him that the pig was in the bathtub before he stepped in.

When we got in the car, Dad was on the phone
with his office. Apparently, there was some sort
of emergency, and he was the only one who knew
how to take care of it.

Mom had planned a big day for us with lots of
stops, so she wasn't happy that Dad had to deal
with a work situation. But we hit the road anyway,
and Dad talked on the phone while he drove.

Our first stop was a place that claimed to have the largest piece of popcorn in the world, which ended up not being that impressive. First of all, it wasn't a real piece of popcorn — it was a wood carving. And, second, it wasn't even all that big.

When we got out of the car, Dad stayed back on his call. The pig stayed, too, sleeping off the drinks from the minibar.

Next we went to a place that's supposedly "world famous" because it has life-size carvings of all the US presidents in butter.

112

This time Mom made Dad get out of the van and join us, but he stayed on the phone the whole time.

When we got back in the car, Mom let Dad know it wasn't OK for him to be missing out on "family time". Dad told her he just needed to deal with one more work issue and, after it was taken care of, he'd give us his full attention.

Dad said he was about to get a call from one of his international clients and that when he DID it was really important for everyone to stay quiet so it would seem like Dad was in the office.

It didn't look like that was gonna be a big problem.
Manny was already down for his afternoon nap,
and the pig was still passed out in the cooler.

A few minutes later, Dad's call came in. You could
tell by how loud the guy was talking that he was
upset. But Dad spoke in an even tone, and his
client seemed to calm down.

The rest of us stayed as quiet as we could. But
then Rodrick got out one of his packs of bubble
gum and put all five pieces in his mouth and
started chewing it real loud.

Mom snapped her fingers to try to get him to
stop making so much noise.

But her finger snapping was actually LOUDER than the gum chewing, which you could tell was irritating Dad.

Mom wanted Rodrick to get rid of his gum, so she pressed the button to open the sunroof. But when she DID the sound of air blowing inside the van was like a jet turbine.

Mom realized she had made a mistake, so she pressed the button to CLOSE the sunroof. But, before it shut all the way, Rodrick chucked his gum through the opening.

The gum boomeranged right BACK and got stuck in the gear track of the sunroof.

Mom frantically pressed the "close" button, but the sunroof was jammed open. At that moment, the air rushing in from outside dislodged Flat Stanley from the vent, and he went flying.

Dad was having a really hard time concentrating on his call and was fumbling with the buttons to try to shut the sunroof himself.

But now he didn't have a hand on the wheel and was steering with his KNEES.

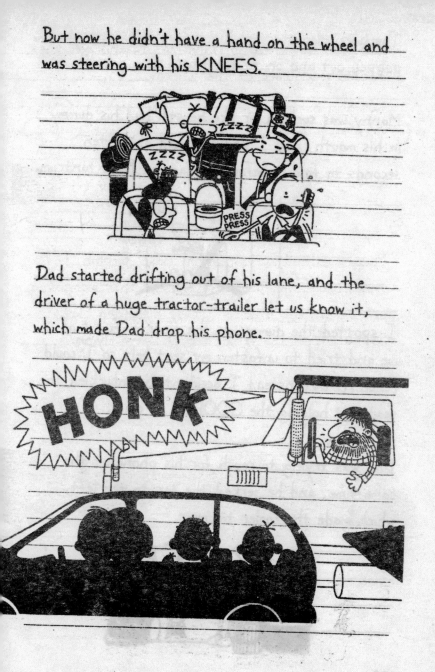

Dad started drifting out of his lane, and the driver of a huge tractor-trailer let us know it, which made Dad drop his phone.

The horn also startled Manny, and his dummy popped out and on to the floor.

Manny was sucking air like he still had his dummy in his mouth, and I knew we had about ten seconds to find it before he had a full-on tantrum.

I spotted the dummy on the floor in front of me and tried to unfasten my seat belt so I could reach it. But instead I accidentally unbuckled the seat belt holding the COOLER in place.

Dad was trying to reach for his phone at the same time, and he jerked the car to the left, which made the cooler tip over.

Now it was total chaos. The pig was loose, Manny was crying and Dad was cursing because he couldn't reach his phone.

But the main problem was the PIG. It was going bananas, running around on the floor and squealing like crazy. Everyone was trying to grab it, but the pig was too slippery.

Then, all of a sudden, the pig went quiet. And when he popped back up we knew why.

SUCK
SUCK
SUCK

I reached out real slow and plucked Manny's
dummy out of the pig's mouth. And that's when it
BIT me.

I guess the pig decided this was its chance to
make a run for it. It hopped up on Manny's seat
and tried to squeeze through the window, which
was open a crack.

The pig managed to get its head and front legs
out of the window and would've made it ALL the
way out if Mom hadn't jumped over her seat and
grabbed its hind legs.

But when she lunged for the pig she kicked a
button on the stereo, and now we had the Spanish
CD blaring at full volume.

The whole time, Dad was swerving all over the
place. Eventually, Mom got the pig back inside
and closed Manny's window. Dad managed to
pull the van over and turn off the stereo.

It was quiet in the car for a full minute while
everyone caught their breath. Dad was really mad
that we messed up his business call, and he let us
know it.

But he probably should've made sure his phone was off first. Because when he put it to his ear his client was still on the other end.

Tuesday
After Dad's work-call disaster yesterday, he and Mom had a long talk outside the car. Then they got back in, and we drove in silence for a while.

Half an hour later, we pulled into the parking lot of a petting zoo. Mom opened the side door and took the cooler with the pig in it out of the van.

Mom went inside, and five minutes later she came out with an empty cooler.

Personally, I wasn't sad to see the pig go, but Manny was a different story.

I'm not so sure Mom was doing the petting zoo any favours by donating a pig that bites kids.

And, speaking of which, my finger was really KILLING me.

Dad said that the pig probably hadn't had any immunizations and might even have rabies, which was NOT what I wanted to hear.

I've seen enough horror movies to know that when a person gets bitten by an animal nothing good comes of it. The LAST thing I need is to turn into some kind of were-pig, because that could really mess up my dating life.

Mom took a look at my finger, and I could tell she was a little worried. She said we should find a doctor to check it out, which didn't calm my nerves any.

Mom tried to find an emergency-care place on the GPS, but there was nothing within a fifty-mile radius.

But she DID find a VETERINARIAN'S office
five minutes up the road.

She said a veterinarian would have the same stuff
as a regular doctor, but a vet could actually be
BETTER because they might know a thing or
two about pig bites.

I honestly thought Mom was joking around about
this veterinarian thing, but she was dead serious.
And a few minutes later we pulled into the
parking lot.

Mom talked to the receptionist at the front desk
while the rest of us waited on a bench.

A minute later, Mom came back with a clipboard
and some paperwork to fill out.

All I can say is I hope this stuff doesn't get
filed on my permanent record, because if it crops
up later in life it could be embarrassing.

Emergency Pet Care

Patient Registration

Pet's name: "Greg"

Owner's name: Susan Heffley

Species: Human

Last vaccination: January 12

History of worms? Yes ☒ No ☐

as a toddler
~~Last rabies shot:~~ N/A

Spayed/Neutered? Yes ☐ No ☒

Once Mom handed in the forms, the receptionist told me I could sit with the other "patients" to wait for the doctor.

You'd think I'd get some sort of priority because I'm a human being, but I got put behind a gerbil that had swallowed a cigarette and a cat that had got its face stuck in a yogurt container.

When we had our dog, Sweetie, Mom had to take him to the vet a bunch of times for getting into stuff he wasn't supposed to eat. But the LAST time she took him she didn't really need to.

Mom had found some empty cellophane wrappers from a pack of whoopie pies in the laundry room, and she figured Sweetie had eaten them.

Apparently, chocolate is like POISON to a dog, so Mom rushed him to the vet to get his stomach pumped.

When Mom brought Sweetie home from the vet, she told me he had got into the whoopie pies. I felt kind of bad, because I was the one who ate them, not the dog.

And, from what I've heard, getting your stomach pumped isn't a real pleasant experience.

I OWE YOU ONE!

I feel like my visit to the vet was payback for the whoopie-pie incident, especially when the nurse weighed me on the same scale they use for DOGS.

The nurse took my temperature, too, and had me hold the thermometer under my tongue for thirty seconds.

When I got back to the waiting area, Rodrick told me that when they take an ANIMAL'S temperature they stick the thermometer somewhere ELSE, and they probably use the same one for all their patients.

I was worried Rodrick might be right, but then
I realized this information was coming from a guy
who was eating gerbil pellets.

Twice while we were waiting at the vet's, Manny
bolted out of the front door, and both times
Dad grabbed him before he got too far. I
think Manny was pretty mad about us leaving his
pig at the petting zoo, and he was acting out.

When I was Manny's age, I used to get mad at
Mom and Dad and try to run away all the time.

I remember once when we were in the changing room at the pool and Mom was trying to make me wear a bathing suit I didn't like. I took off running, but I wasn't really thinking about where I was GOING.

RODRICK used to run away a lot, too. When he was in first grade, he'd take off every day at the same time, but he'd come back home when Mom told him his favourite TV show was on.

When Manny tried to run away a THIRD time today, Mom bought a retractable leash at the front desk to try to keep him under control.

Mom also got a bandage for Rodrick's foot so we could start going into restaurants as a family again.

Finally, the veterinarian was ready to see me, and the nurse led us into the exam room. My palms started getting sweaty, because I always get a little nervous when it's time to see the doctor.

I'm not a big fan of needles, and Mom knows it. So whenever I need to get a flu shot or something Mom doesn't tell me it's coming.

And by the time I figure out what's going on it's too late.

But there weren't any shots this time round. Mom told the vet what had happened, and she took a look at my finger.

The vet said there was nothing to worry about since the pig's teeth hadn't broken the skin.

She put some antibacterial ointment on my finger just to be safe and then sent me on my way.

I gotta say, I was pretty impressed by the whole veterinarian experience. The doctor was no-nonsense and didn't ambush me with any needles.

I figure when we get back home I might research some veterinarians in our area. I'm not saying I'm definitely going to make the switch, but I do want to see what my options are.

After the vet's, Dad spent some time trying to get the gum out of the sunroof with a popsicle stick. But it was too messy and eventually he gave up.

ARAGE

Dad didn't like not being able to close the sunroof, so he drove around trying to find a mechanic who could fix it. But nobody he talked to would do it for under a hundred bucks.

So Dad went to a grocery store and bought some cellophane and duct ta , and he fashioned his OWN sunroof.

STRETCH

I think Dad was pretty proud of himself for saving money on repairs, especially when it started to rain and his homemade sunroof held up.

But after a while the cellophane started filling with water and bugs.

Eventually, the whole thing gave way, and for once I was glad to be sitting in the back.

We parked under an overpass and waited for the rain to clear up while Manny and Rodrick changed into some dry clothes.

The trip was a total disaster up to this point, and even Mom was ready to admit it.

She said it probably wasn't such a good idea to do everything according to the magazine, and that if we switched things a little maybe we could turn the trip around.

Mom said that from then on we'd go wherever the road took us and we'd make decisions as a FAMILY along the way. She said the rest of the trip could be like those Choose Your Own Adventure books.

I always liked those books, because on every page you get to make a decision that changes the story.

The ancient statue has a priceless gem in its eye socket. The inscription at the base of the statue reads STEAL FROM ME AND PERISH. What do you do?

If you prise the gem from the statue, turn to page 40.

If you stop and pet the kitten, turn to page 23.

93

The problem is I never seem to make the choices that get me to a happy ending.

In fact, it seems like no matter WHAT choice I make it's always the WRONG one.

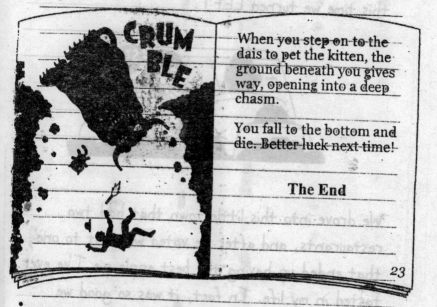

CRUMBLE

When you step on to the dais to pet the kitten, the ground beneath you gives way, opening into a deep chasm.

You fall to the bottom and die. Better luck next time!

The End

23

I wasn't so sure about Mom's new approach, but I figured anything was an improvement as long as I didn't get bitten by any more pigs.

After the rainstorm passed, we got back in the car and gave Mom's idea a try. When we reached our first intersection, she asked everyone if we should turn right or left or go straight.

So we held a vote. Me and Rodrick voted to turn right, and that's what we did. And when we got to ANOTHER intersection we voted again, and this time we turned LEFT.

We drove into this little town that had two restaurants, and after we voted we went to one that ended up having the best apple pie I've ever tasted in my life. In fact, it was so good we ordered a SECOND one.

Mom was really pleased with herself for coming up with this new approach and said she was gonna write in to "Family Frolic" and tell THEM about it.

The only person who WASN'T having a good time was MANNY, who still seemed upset about the pig. Mom kept the leash on him even while we were eating, to make sure he didn't try to run away again.

After lunch, Mom asked me to take Manny to the bathroom, which only had one toilet in it. So I waited outside for him to do his business.

Manny was in there for a while, and I started to wonder what was taking him so long.

I finally opened the door, and he was GONE.

Luckily, Dad saw Manny through the front window of the restaurant and scooped him up before it was too late. Because, if it had been another minute or two, who knows HOW far he would've got.

We got back in the van and Mom strapped Manny into his car seat. When we got to a stoplight, everyone agreed that we should go left, and we waited for the light to change.

When it turned green, Dad stepped on the accelerator, but a car came out of nowhere and TOTALLY ran the red light.

Dad laid on the horn, but the driver just kept on going.

Then another car ran the light, and then ANOTHER. It was like nobody even NOTICED that the light was red.

Dad was getting pretty frustrated, and when he saw a gap between two cars he put the pedal to the floor and hung a left.

We barely squeezed in front of the NEXT car, which ALSO ran the light.

When I looked back at the car behind us, I noticed something weird. There was a little flag on either side of the hood.

Mom noticed the flags, too, and she got really upset. She said the vehicles behind us were part of a FUNERAL procession.

She explained that during a funeral cars are allowed to go through red lights on their way from the church to the cemetery so they can all stick together. And now we'd gone and cut off the line of cars.

Dad was getting panicky that all the cars behind our van were now following US, and he tried to shake them off our tail by making a few quick turns.

It didn't work, though. Dad said he was gonna get back on the highway and try to lose the cars THAT way, but Mom said the LEAST we could do was lead the people behind us to the cemetery.

So Mom typed "cemetery" into the GPS, and there was one just a few blocks away.

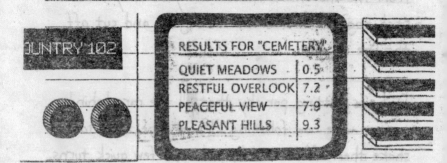

RESULTS FOR "CEMETERY"	
QUIET MEADOWS	0.5
RESTFUL OVERLOOK	7.2
PEACEFUL VIEW	7.9
PLEASANT HILLS	9.3

We drove through the gates and parked along the side of the path. Everyone who was following us got out of their cars, but they seemed confused.

One look at the gravestones and it was clear what had happened. Apparently, the GPS treats all cemeteries the same, and it had taken us to a PET cemetery.

Luckily, Dad got us out of there before things got ugly.

After escaping with our lives from the pet cemetery, everyone decided it would be best to just pack it in for the night. So we found a hotel a few miles away and got a room on the seventh floor.

Dad wasn't comfortable leaving all our stuff in the van, since someone could get in through the sunroof and steal whatever they wanted, so we had to take EVERYTHING into the hotel.

This morning Mom wanted to keep going with the Choose Your Own Adventure plan. I was starting to wonder if it was such a great idea, since it almost got us killed yesterday, but Mom was sticking with it.

She grabbed a bunch of brochures from the front desk and brought them to breakfast so we could figure out what we wanted to do for the day.

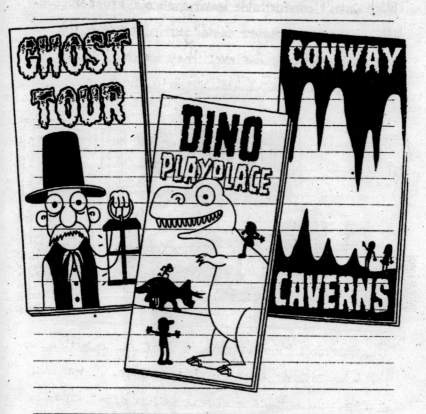

There were actually TOO many options, and
nobody could agree on what to do.

Dad wanted to take an all-day guided tour of a
Civil War battlefield. Mom wanted to go to the
beach. And Rodrick wanted to go to the electric-
guitar museum.

What looked like the most fun to ME was a place
called Soak Central. We went to a water park
LAST summer but got rained out, so I figured
this would make up for it.

But Mom read through the brochure and said Soak
Central looked "artificial" and that the whole
point of this trip was to AVOID places like that.

Since nobody could agree on anything, Mom said she was making an "executive decision" and that we were going to the beach. Dad didn't complain, because I'm sure he was thinking that if we were going to the shore he might actually get a chance to use his BOAT.

I'm really not much of a beach person myself. Whenever we go to one, we bring a blanket and spread it out, then sit there for the whole day. And you can't really go anywhere, because you're worried someone will take your spot.

PAT
PAT

The last time we went to the beach, Dad brought the tarp he uses to cover the boat so we'd have more room for our family and all our stuff.

But the tarp was at LEAST twice the size of our old blanket, and it took up a ton of space on the beach.

Not to mention the fact that it's made of PLASTIC, so, with the sun beating down, it was like sitting in a frying pan.

It was ESPECIALLY embarrassing when the rest of my family went to grab lunch on the boardwalk and I had to hang back on the tarp by myself to watch our stuff.

So I wasn't real excited about going to the beach, especially since I knew Dad had his boat tarp with him.

The beach was a few hours' drive away, so I decided to take a nap until we got there. And, believe me, with all the junk piled up in the back of the minivan, it wasn't easy.

I woke up when the van slowed down. I thought we were at the beach, but we hadn't even got to the bridge yet. It seemed like everyone had the same idea WE did.

HONK HONNK BEEEEP

When we were about a quarter of a mile from
the bridge, I could tell Dad was starting to
get nervous.

He HATES bridges, because for some reason he
gets dizzy whenever he has to drive over one.

The bridge to the beach is one of those kinds
that's really high above the water, and I'm sure
Dad wasn't looking forward to being stuck on it
for the next half hour.

Mom told Rodrick HE could drive. So we pulled
over and everyone switched seats.

Dad took my place in the back so he wouldn't see the bridge out of the front window, and I moved to the middle row.

When Rodrick got in the driver's seat, he took advantage of Dad's radio rule and blasted heavy-metal music. And I could tell that wasn't helping Dad's nerves.

We were only going about three miles an hour. It looked like we were gonna be stuck on the bridge even longer than I expected, so I opened the bag of cheese curls Rodrick bought at the grocery store.

There was a seagull sitting on the bridge railing next to our minivan, and it looked right at me.

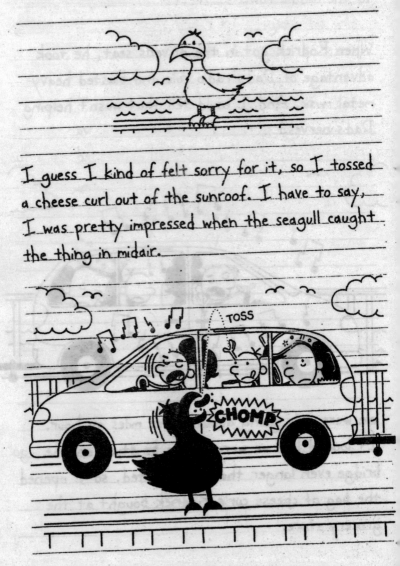

I guess I kind of felt sorry for it, so I tossed a cheese curl out of the sunroof. I have to say, I was pretty impressed when the seagull caught the thing in midair.

I was about to throw it ANOTHER one, but
Mom stopped me.

She said seagulls are really aggressive, and giving
them "people food" is a bad idea.

She was right about the "aggressive" thing,
because two seconds later the seagull was on top
of the car, and you could tell it wanted more food.

I threw another one at it to try to make it go
away, but the seagull bobbled the cheese curl,
which fell right back into the car.

That's when things got BAD.

"The seagull hopped down INTO the car and ate the cheese curl off the floor.

For a second, everyone was in a state of shock that a seagull was in our van, and nobody moved a muscle.

The seagull squawked a few times and then tried to fly back out the way it came in. But it missed the opening by about two feet and smacked into the roof.

Then it just went completely nuts, flying around and crashing into the windows. Everyone was in a total panic, and feathers and cheese curls were everywhere.

Then the seagull got greedy and grabbed the bag of cheese curls off the floor. But I snagged it and held on for dear life. Everyone was yelling at me to let go of the bag, but I wasn't giving in.

Finally, the seagull beat me in our tug-of-war and flew straight up through the sunroof, taking the cheese curls with it. But the seagull didn't get far with the bag.

About three-quarters of the cheese curls ended up BACK in the minivan, and from there it was a total nightmare.

A few of the seagulls flew up front, and Rodrick got so freaked out he hit the accelerator. When the birds finally cleared out and things settled down, we had a whole NEW problem to deal with.

HISSSS

Believe it or not, the people in the car that we rear-ended were actually pretty nice.

It was a man and his wife, and they seemed to understand it was an accident. So they exchanged insurance information with Dad, and the police didn't even need to get involved.

If anything GOOD came out of the accident, it was that it got us out of going to the beach.

The BAD news was that now our van wouldn't start, and we had to wait an hour for a tow truck to come.

All the traffic went down to one lane, and that didn't make us too popular with the people trying to cross the bridge.

The guy at the auto-repair shop said we cracked the radiator and it was gonna take at least four or five hours to fix it. That meant we needed to find something to do for the rest of the day.

When we stepped outside, I was pretty shocked to find out we were only two blocks away from Soak Central, which is where I wanted to go in the FIRST place.

I BEGGED Mom to let us go there while we were waiting for the van to get fixed.

She said she would rather we did something "wholesome" like go to a local library, but this time she was outvoted four to one.

So we walked to Soak Central and paid for tickets at the gate. Then we got a locker, and put in all the stuff that we didn't want to get wet.

We changed into our bathing suits and met outside the restrooms. It was SUPER crowded, and there was no way we were gonna find five lounge chairs all together. We eventually found ONE chair with a few broken straps, and dumped our towels and the rest of our stuff on it.

Mom and Dad stayed back with Manny, so me and Rodrick were on our own. But Mom said she wanted the two of us to stick together.

STRAIN

We went to the giant wave pool first, but there were about a BILLION people in it.

Rodrick suggested we play hide-and-seek, but, with all the people and rafts in the pool, I knew it would be impossible for the seeker to find the hider.

I said to make it FAIR the hider couldn't swim underwater. I didn't really trust Rodrick not to cheat, but he came up with a way to make sure the hider followed the rules.

Rodrick got a paper place mat from the snack bar and said the hider had to keep it dry to prove he didn't go underwater. And I have to admit I was pretty impressed he came up with that all on his own.

I volunteered to be the first hider and found a spot at the far end of the pool where I knew Rodrick would have trouble finding me.

What I DIDN'T know was that Rodrick had written something on the place mat before giving it to me. Unfortunately, everyone AROUND me noticed before I did.

What he wrote would've been bad enough on its OWN, but the misspelled word somehow made it WORSE.

I am not waring a bathing suit

And even MORE embarrassing was when the lifeguard got down from her chair and told me I had to get out of the pool.

When it comes to Rodrick, I've gotta learn never to trust him. ESPECIALLY at water parks.

I was done with Rodrick after the place-mat
thing and didn't care if Mom said we needed to
stick together. I left him behind and went to a
waterslide by myself.

I hadn't realized how long the line was until I
got halfway up the stairs. But by then a ton
of people were BEHIND me, and there was no
turning back. So I was packed in with these
people until I got to the top.

SMOOCH

It was really hot, and people were starting to
get agitated by how slowly the line was moving.

Then the kid right behind me poked the lady in FRONT of me in the butt with a pool noodle, and she thought it was ME.

So then I had her BOYFRIEND to deal with.

I really didn't want to get into a fight over something like this, but luckily it didn't come to that. We were at the top of the stairs, and it was time to go down the slide.

Unfortunately, the raft was a four-seater, which made things pretty awkward on the ride down.

The slide emptied out into an area where there were a ton of rafts, which was great because it gave me a chance to hide from that woman and her boyfriend. I went round the lazy river twice to make sure I'd lost them.

I'd had enough with the water after that, so I went back to our lounge chair to get my clothes.

But the chair was GONE, and all our stuff was lying in a pile on the ground.

I found the rest of my family at the snack bar getting lunch and told them what happened with our lounge chair.

SNACK BAR

ICE CREAM

Mom said it wouldn't be hard to figure out who TOOK it because of the broken straps.

172

We spread out to look for it, and I searched the area by the wave pool.

Sure enough, our lounge chair was there. But I couldn't BELIEVE who was SITTING in it.

I don't know what the odds are of running into the same people again and again, but this was starting to get RIDICULOUS.

I figured it was best to just let the Beardos HAVE our lounge chair and not make it into a big deal. So, when I caught back up with my family, I pretended I didn't have any luck finding our chair.

By now our food was getting cold, and we still didn't have anywhere to eat. We eventually found a place to sit behind the snack bar.

Everyone seemed ready to leave after that. Mom asked for the key to the locker so she could get our stuff. But I told her I didn't HAVE it.

She said she had given me the key, but I turned both pockets of my bathing suit inside out to prove they were empty.

I was pretty sure she'd given the key to RODRICK, but he said HE didn't have it, either.

Everybody searched themselves for the key, but we all came up empty-handed. This was a HUGE problem, because Mom and Dad's phones and wallets were in that locker, so we couldn't leave until we found it.

We went to an employee at the front counter and told him we lost our key.

But when he asked what our locker number was none of us could remember. There were hundreds of them, and they all looked exactly the same.

He said the locker number was written on the key, but of course THAT information wasn't getting us anywhere.

The guy said the only thing we could do was try to FIND the key, so we split up and retraced our steps across the water park.

Rodrick went to the wave pool where we'd played hide-and-seek, and I went to the lazy river but didn't have any luck.

When we met back up, nobody had found the key. Mom said maybe we accidentally threw it away after we ate, so we dug through the trash near where we sat.

Mom said we should all concentrate real hard and try to remember which locker we put our stuff in and, when I did, I could suddenly see it clearly in my mind.

929

930

I told Mom, and we went straight to locker 929. Sure enough, it was locked, and there was no key in the door.

We went back to the guy at the counter to tell him which locker was ours, but we had to wait a long time before we could get his attention.

When we told him our locker number, he got out the master key and walked over to number 929 with us. But by the time we got there the key was back in the slot and the locker was EMPTY.

That meant someone had found our key and STOLEN all our stuff.

Then I thought of ANOTHER possibility: when the Beardos took our lounge chair, they must've taken our KEY, too.

I decided to tell Mom and Dad all about the Beardos and how they probably stole our stuff to get some payback on me. Then I took them to the area where I last saw them sitting.

But when we got there they were GONE.

I was worried they might've already left the park, so I ran to the front gate. And, sure enough, the purple van was pulling away.

I KNEW that family was bad news from the beginning, but I never thought they were capable of THEFT.

Dad used the phone at the front desk to call the police, but the cops said that without a licence-plate number it would be really hard to track down our stolen stuff.

If there was any GOOD news about our situation, it was that the key to the van wasn't in the locker, because it was back at the mechanic's.

So we walked to the auto-repair shop, where the mechanic was getting ready to put in a new radiator. He told Dad it was gonna cost almost three hundred dollars, but Dad told him he couldn't pay because his wallet just got stolen.

Dad told the mechanic he'd mail him a cheque the second we got home, but the guy said he couldn't take an "IOU". He said what he COULD do was put some sealant on the busted radiator, which would last a day or two before it wore off.

But the mechanic said we'd have to run the heater inside the van at full blast to keep the engine from overheating. He said it might sound crazy, but it actually works.

Mom and Dad talked it over and decided we should just drive the van all the way home. We didn't have any money or a phone, but we DID have a full tank of petrol. Dad figured if we drove straight through we'd get back at about 3:00 in the morning.

Mom seemed pretty sad the trip was getting cut short, but, to be honest, I was kind of relieved.

When we got in the van, Dad turned up the heat just like the mechanic told him to, and within about thirty seconds it was a hundred degrees inside the car.

Mom opened all the windows up front, but it was like a FURNACE where I was sitting, since the windows back there don't open.

I told Mom I didn't think I could make it all the way home without dying of heatstroke, but she said I'd be fine as long as I stayed hydrated. Then she got two cases of water out of the boat and brought them into the van.

We headed out on to the highway, and I went through four bottles of water in the first hour.

I tried to fall asleep to make the trip go faster, but I got woken up when somebody started honking their horn.

The people in the car next to us were waving their arms and trying to get our attention.

When I looked behind us, I was surprised to see that the tarp on the boat was loose and flapping around in the wind.

And everything INSIDE the boat was flying OUT.

Cars were swerving left and right, trying to avoid our stuff flying through the air. By now, Dad had seen what was going on in the rear-view mirror, and he pulled over to the side of the road.

We spent the next two hours walking down the highway trying to recover all of our stuff. But we had to give up when it got dark.

Once we got back to the van, we sorted through the things we had collected. I'd say I found about two-thirds of the clothes I'd packed for the trip, but Mom said there were whole BAGS that were missing.

What was REALLY gross was that a few of the items we picked up weren't even OURS. Rodrick found a pair of underwear that was as stiff as cardboard.

Once we got back in the car, Mom said we needed to start thinking about eating. Rodrick wanted to open the package of cinnamon rolls that was still in the grocery bag, but Mom said they hadn't been refrigerated and he'd get sick if he ate them.

Mom used the GPS to try to find a place to eat. But the only places that were open at that hour were fast-food restaurants, and Mom wasn't happy about that.

We ended up pulling over at a rest stop along the highway that had a fried chicken place. Since we didn't have any cash or credit cards, we had to scrounge around on the floor of the car for loose change.

We came up with three dollars and fifteen cents, which I was pretty sure wasn't even enough to get a drumstick and a thigh.

Mom said maybe they had a value menu with less expensive items, so we got out of the car and walked to the restaurant.

But, when we got to the entrance, the doors were locked. We could see workers inside, but apparently at that hour the only thing open was the drive-through.

We got back in the car and tried to enter the drive-through lane, but with the boat it was too tight a squeeze. So we had to repark and go through on FOOT.

We stood next to the menu and waited for someone to come on the speaker and take our order, but no one did.

Dad said there must be some kind of sensor that could detect the weight of a car, so we did our best to trigger it.

Eventually, somebody inside noticed us and opened the drive-through window.

Mom asked what we could get with the money we had, and the cashier said we could buy a small box of chicken nuggets and a couple of cookies.

So we got that, plus a handful of barbecue-sauce packets. Then we went back to the van and split the food five ways.

We drove for a half hour or so, but by now it was pretty obvious we weren't gonna make it all the way home in one shot. So we were gonna have to find a place to sleep.

We didn't have any money for a hotel, so Mom tried to find a campsite nearby.

The closest one was ten miles in the opposite direction, though. Dad said we were just gonna have to take the next exit, find a place where we could park and sleep in the car.

I was open to just about anything as long as we could turn the heater off when we stopped.

But, as soon as we took the exit, it was clear we'd made a mistake.

First of all, the road wasn't paved. There weren't any petrol stations or stores or even any houses. There were just trees on either side of the road and no streetlights.

We drove for a long time, but the road was narrow and there wasn't a good place to pull over. I think everyone was getting pretty spooked, and eventually Mom told Dad we should just get back on the highway.

But Dad kept saying he was POSITIVE that at any moment we were gonna find a good place to stop.

The further we went, though, the more nervous Mom became, because now even the GPS didn't know where we were.

We saw some signs up ahead, and we all got excited that maybe we were getting back to civilization. But we were wrong.

Right at the moment when everyone's nerves were totally shot, there was a really loud noise.

Dad swerved off the road, and our car came to a stop in the mud.

My ears were ringing, and I looked around to try to figure out what had happened.

I expected to see broken glass everywhere, but the windows were intact, and there was some kind of weird goo all over them.

Rodrick had the gooey stuff on the back of his head, and he was TOTALLY freaking out.

I still didn't know what was going on, but then I looked in the grocery bag, which had shreds of the cinnamon-roll package inside.

The tube had EXPLODED because the bag was sitting right on top of one of the heater vents.

but RODRICK didn't know that yet. He had uncooked cinnamon rolls all over the back of his head, and he thought the dough was his BRAINS.

What upset Rodrick even MORE was when he saw Manny licking the stuff off his fingers.

Once Rodrick figured out what had happened and calmed down, we cleaned up the inside of the minivan with some paper towels.

Then Dad turned the car round and drove back to the highway. At the next exit there was a supermarket with an empty parking lot, so Dad pulled in for the night.

We only had four reclining seats in the van and five people, so Mom volunteered Dad to sleep in the boat.

I know Dad was looking forward to using his boat on this trip, but I'm guessing this was NOT what he had in mind.

<u>Wednesday</u>

It took me a long time to fall asleep last night, and I was woken up at about 6:00 in the morning when the supermarket employees started arriving for work.

By then the sun was up and it was already hot in the car, plus we were all sticky and miserable from sleeping in our clothes.

We walked over to the supermarket to see if they'd let us use the restrooms to wash up, but the manager said the store wouldn't be open to customers for another two hours.

When we were walking back to the car, Mom said we could use Manny's baby wipes to get cleaned up. But then she realized she had accidentally locked the keys inside the minivan.

There was HOPE, though. The sunroof was still open, so Dad tried to FISH the keys out of the cup holder.

After a lot of trying, he still couldn't get the right angle. It looked like we were out of options at that point, but then Mom suggested maybe MANNY could get the keys out.

So Dad lowered Manny through the sunroof by his leash.

Once Manny was in the van, he took his sweet time. First he went to the back and ate the two barbecue-sauce packets we had left. Then he dug through my duffel bag and found a pack of Oreos I'd been saving just in case.

199

Manny finally made his way to the front of the car and got the keys, but, instead of opening the door to let us in, he started the ENGINE.

Then he fiddled with the knob on the stereo until he found a radio station he liked.

♫ THE ITSY-BITSY ♪ SPIDER CLIMBED UP ♪ THE WATERSPOUT ♫

Mom and Dad were pounding on the windows, trying to get Manny to open the door. But then Manny put the car in DRIVE.

I think until then everyone had forgotten that Manny had been trying to run away, because we never would've made the mistake of letting him in the van by himself if we had remembered.

Luckily, Manny wasn't tall enough to reach the accelerator, because, if he could, he would've been long gone.

I think Manny knew his escape plan was foiled, at least for now. Mom finally convinced him to unlock the doors and let us in.

Once we got going again, I started seeing some familiar sights out of the window, because we were basically retracing our path back home.

We were coming up to the town where we'd spent the first night of the trip, and when we passed by the motel we'd stayed in I saw the CRAZIEST thing.

There was a purple van in the parking lot.

I told Dad, and he pulled over. We took a closer look at the van and, sure enough, it was the one that belonged to the Beardos.

That meant they were staying at THIS motel, and were probably using Mom and Dad's credit cards to PAY for it.

We parked our car at the side of the building. Dad said he was gonna call the cops, so he got out to use the phone at the front desk.

But thirty seconds later Dad came running back to the car.

He said he saw the Beardos leaving their room to go down to the pool, and it looked like their door was left open.

Mom said we should stick with the plan and call the police, but Dad said that before we did we should do a little investigation of our OWN.

So we ALL got out and followed Dad to the Beardos' room. Just like he said, the door was open a crack.

Dad nudged it open a little WIDER, and we peeked inside to see if anything of ours was sitting in plain view.

But we couldn't see any of our stuff from where we were standing.

Mom seemed pretty uneasy about what we were doing, but then Dad pushed the door ALL the way open, and there was no turning back.

TOSS

We couldn't find anything of ours, so if the
Beardos DID have any of our stuff they probably
carried it with them to the pool.

But as long as we had the run of their room we
decided to take full advantage of it. I figured
it was OK since we were the ones paying for it.

I think Mom felt we were setting a bad example for
Manny, so she took him out to the car.

But the rest of us weren't finished. Me and
Rodrick took turns using the bathroom while Dad
stood watch at the door.

Then he went in and told us to be lookouts for HIM.

We had pushed our luck, though. The SECOND
Dad shut the door to the bathroom, I saw the
Beardos coming our way.

Now, I love my dad and all, but I'm too YOUNG
to die. So I bolted, and Rodrick was right
behind me.

I wasn't there to SEE it, but I'm guessing it
was pretty awkward when Mr Beardo opened his
bathroom door.

Me and Rodrick got in the van and locked the doors. I was pretty convinced Dad wasn't gonna make it out of the room alive and we were just gonna have to go on without him.

But Mom pulled the car round to the front of the motel, and when she did Dad burst out of the Beardos' room.

Somehow Dad had got the idea to grab their car keys on his way out.

Before he got in our car he chucked the keys into some bushes, which bought us some time.

I think we must've gone two miles down the road before Dad even bothered to pull his trousers back up.

We high-fived each other because we had escaped with our lives. But, in our rush to get away, we forgot to turn on the HEATER.

And a few seconds later the RADIATOR conked out.

Mom had to cut across two lanes of traffic to get the van into the breakdown lane. But in the spot where we pulled over there was a broken bottle, and we rolled right over it.

We got out of the car so we could change the tyre. Dad opened the back hatch to find his jack, but unfortunately I had taken it out before we left for the trip to make room for my PILLOW.

The only thing we could do at that point was wait for help to come.

Eventually, a car pulled over behind us, but when it got closer I knew we were in big trouble.

It was a purple van.

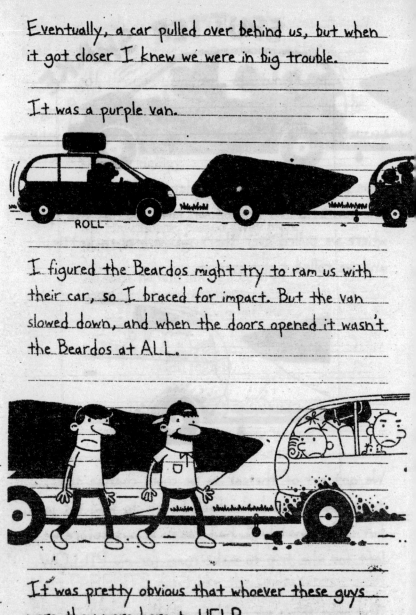

I figured the Beardos might try to ram us with their car, so I braced for impact. But the van slowed down, and when the doors opened it wasn't the Beardos at ALL.

It was pretty obvious that whoever these guys were they were here to HELP.

But they didn't speak English, so we were having trouble communicating with them. Mom and Dad tried to act out what was wrong with the car, and I'm sure the two guys thought my parents had completely lost their minds.

Then Manny surprised EVERYONE by speaking in perfect Spanish.

The conversation between Manny and the two guys lasted a long time, so I figured Manny was explaining everything that had happened on our trip.

He must've done a good job making the guys feel sorry for us, because, the next thing you knew, they were offering us a RIDE. And I'm happy to say their air-conditioning worked GREAT.

I think we assumed these guys were taking us to a mechanic or something, but we were wrong.

We should've realized that if MANNY was the one doing all the talking we'd end up going where HE wanted to go.

Sunday
Like I said before, Mom was right about pigs being smart. She had it house-trained within a week, and the pig even knows a few tricks already.

My only real complaint is that now I never get a chance to watch my shows on TV, because the pig has figured out how to use the remote.

But I'm gonna let that go, because I don't want to get bitten a second time.

It's taken a while for everything to get back to normal after the trip. Dad had to take a few more days off work to cancel all his credit cards and get new ones.

And tomorrow Mom and Dad are supposed to go out and get new drivers' licences and phones.

Our minivan's been at the mechanic's since it was towed. We gave the BOAT to the drivers who helped us out as a way of saying thanks, which was actually Mom's suggestion.

Mom's been saying that, even though our trip didn't go the way we planned, it was still an adventure. She's been working on an article to send in to "Family Frolic" that I seriously hope does NOT get published.

Mom's also been making a scrapbook, and she asked everyone to contribute a souvenir to put inside.

I was going through the clothes I wore on the trip, and when I picked up my shorts something small fell out on to the floor.

It was the KEY from Soak Central.

I couldn't believe I had the key all along. It turns out I was wrong about the locker number. But I should get SOME credit for being CLOSE.

Now that I have the key, I have a tough decision to make. It feels like a page from one of those Choose Your Own Adventure books.

I figure I have three basic choices. One, I can tell Mom and Dad the truth and deal with the consequences. Two, I can plant the key in RODRICK'S dirty laundry and let HIM take the blame. Or, three, I can flush the key down the toilet and forget this whole thing ever happened.

There's a fourth option that involves the pig, but I haven't worked out the details of THAT one yet.

But like I said before, whenever I have a difficult choice to make, I always seem to pick the wrong one. And, whichever way I go here, it's hard to see this story having a happy ending.

ACKNOWLEDGMENTS

Thanks to my wonderful family for your continued love, support and encouragement.

Thanks to everyone at Abrams for treating every Wimpy Kid book like it's the first. Thanks especially to Charlie Kochman, Michael Jacobs, Jason Wells, Veronica Wasserman, Steve Tager, Susan Van Metre, Jen Graham, Chad W. Beckerman, Alison Gervais, Elisa Garcia, Erica La Sala and Scott Auerbach.

Thanks to all my international publishers for bringing Greg's stories to kids all over the world. I feel very grateful for the friendships I've made over the past few years.

Thanks to Shaelyn Germain and Anna Cesary for everything you do to keep all the balls in the air at the same time.

Thanks to Paul Sennott and Ike Williams for all the great advice.

Thanks to everyone in Hollywood who has worked to bring Greg Heffley to life on the big and small screens. Thanks especially to Sylvie Rabineau, Keith Fleer, Nina Jacobson, Brad Simpson, Ralph Milero, Roland Poindexter, Elizabeth Gabler and Vanessa Morrison.

Thanks to everyone at Poptropica, especially Jess Brallier.

ABOUT THE AUTHOR

Jeff Kinney is a #1 *New York Times* bestselling author and four-time Nickelodeon Kids' Choice Award winner for Favourite Book. Jeff has been named one of *Time* magazine's 100 Most Influential People in the World. He is also the creator of Poptropica, which was named one of *Time* magazine's 50 Best Websites. He spent his childhood in the Washington, D.C., area and moved to New England in 1995. Jeff lives with his wife and two sons in southern Massachusetts, where he is opening a bookstore.